THE THREE BEARS
AND GOLDILOCKS

First published in Great Britain by
HarperCollins Publishers Ltd in 1991
First published in Picture Lions 1992

9 8 7 6 5 4 3 2

Picture Lions is an imprint of the Children's Division,
part of HarperCollins Publishers Limited,
77-85 Fulham Palace Road, Hammersmith,
London W6 8JB

Printed in Great Britain by
BPCC Hazell Books, Paulton and Aylesbury

THE THREE BEARS
AND GOLDILOCKS

RETOLD & ILLUSTRATED BY
JONATHAN LANGLEY

PictureLions

An Imprint of HarperCollins*Publishers*

Once upon a time, there were three bears who lived in a little house in the big wood. There was a great big bear called George, a middle-sized bear called Mavis and a tiny little bear called Brian; but they were better known as Father Bear, Mother Bear and Baby Bear, or The Three Bears.

The Three Bears lived very happily and quietly together in their house which was always tidy. They each had their own things. They had their own food bowls: a big one with daisies on for Father Bear, a middle-sized one with buttercups on for Mother Bear and a little one with rabbits on for Baby Bear.

They had their own chairs: a big one with a high back and arms for Father Bear, a middle-sized one with big cushions for Mother Bear and a little one with rabbits on for Baby Bear. They had their own beds: a big one with a carved headboard for Father Bear, a middle-sized one with a quilted headboard for Mother Bear and a little one with rabbits on for Baby Bear.

One morning, when it was his turn to make breakfast,
Father Bear made a big pot of porridge. When it was
ready, he poured it into the three bowls. It was still too
hot to eat so Father Bear suggested, as it was a sunny
morning, that they all go for a stroll in the woods while
the porridge cooled. After opening all the windows to let
the sun in to warm the house, they set off down the path.

On that same morning there was someone else walking in the big wood. A little girl called Goldilocks was stomping along swatting at butterflies with a stick and kicking the heads off flowers. She was in a bad mood. Her mum had told her off and she'd slammed out of the house without any breakfast.

Goldilocks was feeling very hungry when she suddenly smelled the warm, delicious smell of porridge. She followed the smell with her nose until she came to where The Three Bears' house stood in a sunny clearing.

Goldilocks liked the look
of the house and, when
she peeped through the open
window, she saw three bowls
of porridge on the table.
Goldilocks' empty tummy
grumbled. She wondered
if whoever lived in
the house might like to
share their breakfast
with her, so she
knocked on the door.
There was no reply.
Goldilocks then lifted
the latch to see if the
door was locked. It
wasn't. After looking
around, she opened
the door, stepped
inside, and went
straight for the
bowls of porridge
on the table.

She first tried the biggest
bowl with the most amount
of porridge in it.
 "Oooh!" said Goldilocks.
"Too hot."

Then she tried the
middle-sized bowl.
 "Yuk, too cold!" she said.

Next she tried the little
bowl with the rabbits on.
 "Yum, yum just right," she
said, and quickly ate it all up.

Goldilocks then started to make herself at home.

She tried sitting in the biggest chair but it was
very uncomfortable.

"Too hard," said Goldilocks.

Aaarrggh!

Then she tried the
middle-sized chair.

"Too soft," she said.

Next she tried the little chair.

"Mmm, just right," she said.
She liked this one and wriggled
with glee, so much so that –
CRASH! – the back legs broke
and she fell to the floor.

Picking herself up, and feeling a bit cross, Goldilocks then decided to explore the rest of the house. She went upstairs to the bedroom where she found the three beds.

First she tried lying on the biggest bed.

"Too high," she said.

Then she tried lying on the middle-sized bed.

"Too low," said Goldilocks.

Next she tried the little bed.

"Aaah, just right," she said.

It was so comfortable that she immediately
fell fast asleep.

Very soon The Three Bears returned home from their walk
and were surprised to find the door open. They looked
inside and noticed the bowls of porridge on the table.

"Somebody has been eating my porridge!" said Father Bear in a great, gruff, growling voice.

"Somebody has been eating my porridge!" said Mother Bear in a mellow, middle-sized voice.

"Somebody has been eating my porridge, and has eaten it all up!" cried Baby Bear in a squeaky, little voice.

Then they noticed the chairs had been moved.

"Somebody has been sitting in my chair!"
said Father Bear in a great, gruff, growling voice.

"Somebody has been sitting in my chair!" said Mother Bear in a mellow, middle-sized voice.

"Somebody has been sitting in my chair, and broken it all to bits!" sobbed Baby Bear in a squeaky, little voice, dripping tears on to the floor.

The Three Bears then heard the sound of snoring coming from upstairs.

They tiptoed up the stairs and into the bedroom. They looked at the rumpled beds.

"Somebody has been lying on my bed!"
said Father Bear in a great, gruff, growling voice.

"Somebody has been lying on my bed!" said
Mother Bear in a mellow, middle-sized voice.

"Somebody has been lying on my bed, and she's still there!"
wailed Baby Bear in a squeaky, little voice.

This commotion woke Goldilocks up with a start. Seeing
The Three Bears she screamed.
   "EEEEAAAWWAAAGHH!"

This so frightened The Three Bears that they all flung up their arms and they screamed too.

"EEEEEEAAAAWWWWAAAAGGHH!"

Goldilocks thought she was going to be eaten! She leaped out of bed and dived out of the nearest window. She landed in a blackberry bush, picked herself up, and ran off home as fast as her legs would go.

After The Three Bears got over their shock, Father Bear
made some more porridge, Mother Bear mended Baby
Bear's chair and Baby Bear made the beds.

They lived happily ever after and always locked their door
when they went out, just in case.

Goldilocks never went back to The Three Bears' house. She grew up into a fine young woman and had many adventures, but she never did eat porridge again.

JONATHAN LANGLEY

Jonathan Langley was born in Lancaster in 1952. He studied graphic design and illustration at Liverpool College of Art and the Central School of Art and Design. He also studied bookbinding at Camberwell School of Art.

In 1974 he became a freelance illustrator, working in publishing, editorial, advertising and design. He has illustrated several books for children, including *The Wind in the Willows*, *The Wizard of Oz* and three of Kipling's *Just So Stories*. For HarperCollins he has illustrated *The Collins Book of Nursery Rhymes*, *A Pig Called Shrimp*, written by Lisa Taylor, and a series of collectable hardback fairytales - *The Three Bears and Goldilocks*, *The Story of Rumpelstiltskin*, *Little Red Riding Hood*, *The Three Billy Goats Gruff* and *The Princess and the Frog*. His work is featured at the Chris Beetles Gallery in London.

He lives in the Lake District with his wife, Karen, and their three children, Toby, Holly and Rosita.

~THE EXCITING RANGE OF~
JONATHAN LANGLEY TITLES
PUBLISHED BY HARPERCOLLINS: